The Miss Kitty Mystery

The Adventures of Callie Ann

The Miss Kitty Mystery

Shannon Mason Leppard

BETHANY HOUSE PUBLISHERS
MINNEAPOLIS, MINNESOTA 55438

The Miss Kitty Mystery
Copyright © 1997
Shannon Mason Leppard

Cover illustration by Sergio Giovine
Text illustrations by Toni Auble

Published by Bethany House Publishers
A Ministry of Bethany Fellowship, Inc.
11300 Hampshire Avenue South
Minneapolis, Minnesota 55438

Printed in the United States of America.

Library of Congress Cataloging-in-Publication Data

Leppard, Shannon Mason.
    The Miss Kitty mystery / by Shannon Mason Leppard.
    p.   cm. — (The adventures of Callie Ann ; 4)
    Summary: Callie is upset when her beloved Miss Kitty disappears, and then her friend Jason's cat goes off as well.
    ISBN 1–55661–816–6 (pbk.)
    [1. Cats—Fiction. 2. Christian life—Fiction.] I. Title. II. Series:
Leppard, Shannon Mason. Adventures of Callie Ann ; 4.
PZ7.L5565Mi   1997
[Fic]—dc21ws97–21041

                                                      CIP
                                                      AC

For my wonderful sister-in-law
Debbie F. Mason
and
two wonderful nieces
Cammie N. Mason
and Margaret M. Tate—
I love you lots.
With lots of love and thanks to
John and Gayle and Jake
and
Gail and Shyla

Chapter One

Callie Ann Davies woke up early Friday morning to her cat, Miss Kitty, meowing at the window.

"What are you doing?" Callie asked the very large black cat. "Nothing's out there. Come back to bed. It's too early for us to get up."

Callie pulled her sunflower quilt over her head. But Miss Kitty was not about to give up. She jumped from the window seat to Callie's bed and tried to get under the quilt with Callie. But Callie just pulled the quilt tight around her and turned over to face the wall.

"Come on, Miss Kitty. I really don't want to get up," Callie said, trying to hide her face. Miss Kitty jumped back to the window seat. But now she wasn't just meowing. She was howling. Callie had never heard her make that kind of noise before.

"OK, Miss Kitty. I'll get up. Boy, what's gotten into you this morning?" Callie pulled on her blue jean shorts and yellow T-shirt.

The whole time, Miss Kitty just ran back and forth between the window seat and the door.

"Come on, missy. I'll let you out now," Callie called back to the cat, who was at the window for the hundredth time. Miss Kitty made one big jump to the bed and another to the nightstand. She passed Callie before Callie even reached the first step.

Miss Kitty was already meowing at the back door when Callie entered the kitchen.

"You better have a good reason for getting me up this early, Miss Kitty. I really didn't sleep good last night, and I still don't feel good."

Miss Kitty had already run out the door and off the porch. She didn't hear a word Callie said.

"Hurry back, Miss Kitty," Callie yelled to the cat, who was now almost to the barn. "I can't go out with you 'cause I don't have my shoes on. And I'd like to go back to bed soon."

Callie sat down in the big green chair by the kitchen door to wait for Miss Kitty to come back in.

The next thing Callie knew, her daddy was carrying her back up the steps to her room. *I must have fallen asleep*, Callie thought.

"It's way too early for you to be up, little one. It's not even seven yet," Daddy said as he put Callie back in her bed. "You were up most of the night coughing. I think you need to sleep awhile longer."

"I know, Daddy. I still don't feel good." Callie pulled up her covers before remembering Miss Kitty. "OH NO! Daddy, Miss Kitty is still out. I've got to go get her or she'll never come back in." She started to climb out of bed.

"Hold on, missy," Daddy said. "I'll go get Miss Kitty. She'll be fine. Remember, she likes me. Even if I am a *boy*."

Callie pulled up the sunflower quilt and began to drift off to sleep. She could hear her daddy calling Miss Kitty at the back door.

❧❧❧

Callie didn't wake up until almost lunchtime.

She could hear her mom calling Miss Kitty.

"I wonder if Mom let her out again," Callie said to herself as she got out of bed.

She took off the T-shirt and shorts she had put on when Miss Kitty got her up so early. She was looking for something else to wear when she heard Mom call Miss Kitty again. So Callie put on her fuzzy yellow robe and went down to the kitchen. Mom was in the middle of the backyard calling for Miss Kitty.

"Mom, do you want me to go get her?" Callie yelled out the back door.

"Oh, you're up, sweetie. Do you feel any better?" Mom joined Callie back on the porch.

"I guess I do. My head hurts, and my ears still feel funny," Callie answered. "Do you want me to get Miss Kitty?"

"Well, honey, you see . . ." Mom faltered. "After you let her out this morning, Miss Kitty disappeared."

Disappeared!

Chapter Two

"OH NO!" Callie began to cry.

"I'm sure she's fine, honey," Mom said. "But after you went back to bed, Daddy couldn't find her. He and David are out looking for her," Mom explained.

"I've got to get dressed. I have to go find her, Mom. What if she's hurt or something?" Callie turned to go back up to her room.

"Now, Callie Ann, calm down. Your daddy will find her. You're still sick and need to stay here. We'll just sit tight and wait for Daddy and David to get back. OK?" Mom sat Callie on her lap in the big green kitchen chair.

"Mom, I can't just do nothing! I have to help

look for her, please. I'll call Jason and have him look for her, too."

Callie got out of her mom's lap and went to her daddy's study to use the phone. She was crying so hard, she almost couldn't remember Jason's phone number.

"Jason, please help me," Callie cried into the phone. "Miss Kitty is gone, and Mom won't let me go out and find her 'cause I've been sick."

"Calm down, Callie. What are you talking about?" Jason said.

"Miss Kitty went out real early this morning. Daddy put me back in bed because I was sick last night. And now she's gone, and I can't go find her," Callie said between sobs.

"I'm still not sure what you're talking about, Callie. I'll come over and you can tell me in person. OK?" Jason asked.

"OK. I'll go back in the kitchen and wait for you," Callie said.

Callie put the phone down. All she could think of was Miss Kitty outside all by herself. She usually stayed out only a few minutes unless Callie was with her.

Jason knocked on the back door just as Callie

came back into the kitchen.

"Come on in, Jason," Mom said. "Callie will be—well, here she is now."

Jason looked confused. "What's going on? What are you crying about?"

"Well, I was sick last night and didn't sleep real well," Callie began. "Miss Kitty wanted to go out real early this morning—around six. So I got up and let her out. I must have fallen asleep in the chair, 'cause Daddy put me back in bed. He was going to let Miss Kitty back in, but he couldn't find her. Now he and David are out looking for her. And Mom won't let me go because I still don't feel good." Callie spilled it all out at once, not even stopping to catch her breath.

"OK. I'll see if I can find her. I'll go get the walkie-talkies so you know where I go. Then you can tell me where to look," Jason suggested and ran out the door.

"Oh, great! That way I can help look for her, too, in a way." Callie hoped it would work.

They had used the walkie-talkies once before when Callie thought that no one had remembered her birthday. They had worked really well, except they were almost caught spying on Callie's mom.

Callie saw Jason come out his door and went to the back porch to wait for him.

"I've got 'em, Cal!" Jason yelled as he crossed the backyard. "My dad is coming. He said he'll help look for Miss Kitty, too."

Mr. Alexander came out of his house and across their backyard to join Jason and Callie. "Don't you worry, Callie. You just sit tight with your mom. Jason and I will look everywhere you want us to look. OK?"

"Yes, sir. Thank you for helping. Daddy and David are out looking, too," Callie said.

Callie watched as Mr. Alexander and Jason rode off down the street on their bikes. When she couldn't see them anymore, she went back into the kitchen. Mom was just sitting down at the kitchen table with a cup of tea.

"Mr. Alexander is going to help look for Miss Kitty, too," Callie said, sitting down at the kitchen table with her.

"You need to eat something. Then you can take a shower. That will help you feel better." Mom kissed the top of Callie's head. "It also might help your hair lie down a little bit."

"OK. Do we have any chicken noodle soup?" Callie asked.

"We sure do," Mom said. "And I made you some toast. You always like that when you have a cold."

"Mom," Callie began. "Do you think Miss Kitty is all right? I really am worried."

Mom set a bowl of chicken noodle soup on the table. "Honey, I can't say for sure that she is all right. But I do feel like she is. I asked God to look after her, and so did Daddy. Everyone is looking for her. So please try not to worry." She smiled. "You eat. I'll keep an ear on the walkie-talkie."

Callie ate her soup without saying much. It was hard trying not to worry about Miss Kitty. She and her best friend, Meghan Johnson, had gotten their cats at the same time. Miss Kitty and Meg's cat, Mr. Kitty, had been born in the church in Greenville. Then the Davies moved here to Cornelius. Callie still missed Greenville, but not as much as she did at first. Right now she missed Miss Kitty more than anyone would ever know. Miss Kitty was her best friend in the whole

world. She told Miss Kitty everything.

Callie finished her soup and went to the back door. She called for Miss Kitty again, hoping she would come running. No such luck. Miss Kitty was nowhere to be seen.

"Callie, honey," Mom called. "You need to come back in. I know it's warm out, but you have a cold and shouldn't be outside just yet. Maybe you'll feel better tomorrow. Then you can go out."

"But, Mom, what if she needs me? What if she's scared?" Callie cried softly.

"I know, honey. All we can do is ask God to look out for her until we can get her back home. Now, you need to head for the shower, Miss Stinky." Mom laughed.

Callie knew her mom was trying to make her feel better by joking around with her. But Callie just didn't feel up to jokes right then.

"I'm going. Will you keep the walkie-talkie in case Jason calls back in?" Callie asked. "And tell him to look down by the creek at the church. We had Miss Kitty there one day last week."

"I will, sweetie," Mom answered.

Chapter Three

Callie went up to her room to find something to put on after she had taken her shower.

"Let's see, jean shorts and a green shirt. That'll do it," she said and went into the bathroom.

The shower felt good. But Callie hurried to get through. She didn't want to be in the shower if Jason called her on the walkie-talkie. She wanted to hear everything he was doing and everywhere he was going in case he saw Miss Kitty.

As soon as she got out, she called downstairs. "Mom, has Jason checked in yet?" Callie asked.

Mom came to the bottom of the steps and called back, "Yes, honey, he has. I told him about the creek, and he said he would look there. He also said he would look over at the school."

"Thank you, Mom. I'll be down in a few minutes. I need to comb my hair."

"Good luck, sweetie. We haven't combed it since yesterday, so you'll have a hard time. Call me if you need help," Mom offered.

Callie's hair was always a problem. *Wild red hair. Why in the world couldn't I have had normal hair?* Callie thought to herself.

It seemed to take forever to get her hair fixed. When Callie finally went back downstairs, David and her daddy were coming in the back door.

"Did you find her, Daddy?" Callie asked, hoping with all her heart that they had.

"No, sweetie, we didn't," Daddy said. "But David said he'd go back out after supper to look."

"Jason and his daddy are looking, too. Maybe after supper I could go with David to look." Callie looked at her mom for permission.

"Well, Callie, I don't think that's a good idea. You still have a little fever. And I don't think the night air would be good for you. Even if it is summer," Mom explained.

Somehow Callie had known what the answer to that question would be even before she asked it. Mom was just looking out for her. But right now, all Callie could think of was finding Miss Kitty and bringing her home.

"Callie, don't worry. I'll go out after we eat. I'll do everything I can to find Miss Kitty," David told his little sister.

For a big brother, Callie thought, *David is all right. A pain sometimes, but he's OK.*

Supper was almost ready when the phone rang. Callie jumped to answer it, hoping it was Jason calling to say they had found Miss Kitty. But it was someone calling for her daddy.

Supper went by slowly. David tried to be funny, but Callie didn't feel like being cheered up. All she could think of was the missing Miss Kitty.

When supper was over, David started out the door to meet Jenni Wilson, his girlfriend. But first he stopped and hugged Callie.

"Callie, please don't worry. I'll try my best to find Miss Kitty," he said, trying to comfort her. "Remember that I love you. Even if you do have more hair than a sheep, and red to boot."

"Thanks, David. I love you, too," Callie said.

As Callie helped her mom clean up the table and put the dishes in the dishwasher, the walkie-talkie starting making a noise.

"Callie, you there? It's Jason," the voice on the walkie-talkie called out.

Callie quickly picked up the radio off the chair by the door.

"I'm here, Jason. What's going on? Where are you?" Callie asked.

"We're in for the night," Jason said. "We didn't find her. Sorry. My dad and I will go back out in the morning if you want."

"That would be nice of you. Maybe I'll feel better and can go, too," Callie said back into the radio. "Thank you, Jason. You're a good friend . . . for a boy. Oh, and Jason, tell your daddy thank you, too."

Callie put the walkie-talkie down and said, "I wish I could go look for her. If I could just do something. Anything."

"Callie," Mom said. "I know of something you can do tonight. Why don't we make a flyer about Miss Kitty? Daddy can make copies at the church. And you can pass them out tomorrow."

That sounded like a good idea to Callie, so she found a piece of paper and wrote down the information.

MISSING CAT
ANSWERS TO MISS KITTY
TWENTY-TWO POUNDS,
LONG BLACK HAIR
PLEASE CALL THE DAVIES
IF YOU HAVE SEEN HER

Callie put their phone number at the bottom.

"That looks real good, Callie," Daddy said. "I'll make the copies first thing tomorrow."

"Thank you, Daddy. I love you." She gave her daddy a hug, then went up to her room.

Sitting on the window seat where she and Miss Kitty loved to curl up, Callie thought of all the places she had taken Miss Kitty.

The school.

Church.

The creek.

The Masons' house.

The Masons' store.

Even to Dr. Aughtry's office.

Almost anywhere in town. Miss Kitty could have gone to any one of those places and not known her way back home.

"Callie, honey," Callie heard her mom say. "Honey, wake up. You need to get in your bed."

Callie had fallen asleep on the window seat. She was dreaming about when Miss Kitty was born in the bell tower back at the church in Greenville.

It had been spring, and all the flowers smelled really good. Miss Kitty's mama had gotten into the church and upstairs to the bell tower without anyone seeing her.

Six kittens were born that warm spring day. Callie had taken Miss Kitty, and Meghan Johnson took Mr. Kitty. Other people in the church had taken the other four. Callie's grandmama had taken the mama cat and named her Midnight. Miss Kitty looked just like her.

"What time is it, Mom? Is David back yet?" Callie rubbed her eyes.

"Well, it's ten o'clock," Mom said. "David is back, but he didn't find Miss Kitty. I'm sorry, honey."

"I don't know if I can sleep without her,

Mom," Callie cried. "I always sleep with her."

"Oh, I think you can, Callie." Mom put Callie in bed and covered her up with her sunflower quilt.

Folding her hands, Callie started her prayers. "Dear God, it's me, Callie. I don't know what to do. Miss Kitty's missing, and no one can find her. Please keep her safe until I can get to her. Please help David or somebody find her. Bless all the people I love and even the people I don't know. Please keep Grandmama and Papa well. Thank you, God. Amen."

Callie was fast asleep in a few minutes. But her dreams went back to Miss Kitty and where she might be.

Chapter Four

Callie woke up to the sun coming in her bed-room window. It was a very bright morning. She looked at her clock beside her bed.

"Nine-thirty. Oh no. I've missed a good part of the morning," Callie said to herself as she rolled out of bed.

Getting dressed, Callie could hear her daddy talking downstairs. It sounded like Jason was in the kitchen with him.

"Daddy," Callie called down the steps, "is that Jason with you?"

"Yes, Callie, it is. He's going back out to look for Miss Kitty," Daddy answered.

"Wait, Jason. I'm coming, too. I just need to brush my hair," Callie said.

"Better sit down, Jason. It could take a while with that hair of hers," Callie heard her daddy say.

Callie came downstairs and found Jason looking at a picture of Miss Kitty. It would go on the flyer Callie had written out the night before.

"You ready to ride?" Callie asked Jason as she pulled on her tennis shoes. "Daddy is going to run copies of that flyer so we can put them up this morning."

"Wait a minute, Miss Callie Ann," Mom said. "You have to eat first. And I want to see if you are still running a fever."

"Mom, I need to find her," Callie whined. "She's been out all night."

"Eat first, then we'll go." Jason pulled Callie down into a kitchen chair.

Mom put the thermometer in Callie's mouth. While they waited, she poured Callie some orange juice and made her some peanut butter toast.

"No fever," Mom said when she looked at the thermometer. "I guess you can go out for a while. Jason, if you don't mind, I'll keep one walkie-talkie here. That way if Callie gets tired I

can come get her. Watch her for me, Jason."
Mom gave Jason a wink.

"Sure. I'll keep this walkie-talkie on my
bike," Jason said as they went out the back door.

Callie didn't like it one bit that Jason would
be looking out for her.

"Come on, Jason. We have a lot of places to
look today." Callie put on her dark blue bike
helmet and took off.

"Where to first, Callie?" Jason asked as he
caught up with her.

"I think we need to look at the school again."
Callie started down the street to the school.

"What makes you think she'd be at the
school?" Jason asked.

"Well, we took her there last week. Maybe
she went back there to look around." Callie
pedaled faster. She felt much better after sleep-
ing most of Friday. Now it was Saturday, and she
needed to find Miss Kitty. The big black cat had
been gone one whole day.

She has to need food and water, Callie
thought as they pulled up at the school.

Mr. Tucker was just coming out. Mr. Tucker

was the principal at the school and Meghan Johnson's uncle.

"Hi, you two! Just can't wait for school to start, can you?" Mr. Tucker called to them. "It won't be long now."

"Hi, Mr. Tucker. I think we can wait for school. Have you seen Callie's cat, Miss Kitty? She's missing," Jason explained. "We had her up here one day last week."

"Why, no, I haven't seen her. But I'll be on the lookout," Mr. Tucker promised.

"Thank you, Mr. Tucker. Please let my mom know if you see her. She has one of Jason's walkie-talkies, and she'll call us if she hears anything," Callie said.

Mr. Tucker waved as Callie and Jason rode off.

"Now where?" Jason asked.

"I think we should go by the church and pick up the flyers. Daddy should be done with them now," Callie said as they rode out of the school parking lot.

"Maybe we should look in the bell tower while we're there," Jason suggested, following Callie to Riverbend Road, where the church was.

"Jason, get real. How could Miss Kitty get into the church and up to the bell tower?" Callie rolled her eyes at Jason. "The doors are always locked unless Daddy is there. And he said he hasn't seen her."

"It was just an idea. Besides, you never know," Jason replied.

"Well, there's no way she could get into the bell tower. The door is always closed."

Callie and Jason found Daddy in the church study. "Hi, Daddy," Callie said. "Are the flyers ready? We're going to hang them up around town."

"Here they are, hot off the press," he said, handing her the warm stack of flyers.

"Thank you, Daddy. We gotta go!" Callie called, hurrying out the door. "Come on, Jason."

"I'm coming. Slow down," Jason said as Callie hopped on her bike. Just then the walkie-talkie crackled. "Wait, Callie. Someone's calling on the walkie-talkie."

"Callie, Jason, are you there?" came Callie's mom's voice.

"We're here, Mrs. Davies," Jason said.

"Mr. Tucker just called," she told them. "He

said after you left the school, he thought he saw a black cat on the playground."

"Oh, Jason, let's go!" Callie said. "Thanks, Mom. We'll go look." Callie turned her bike around and pedaled off. Finally, a clue!

They coasted up to the playground and left their bikes on the sidewalk. "Where do you think she might be?" Jason asked Callie.

"I don't know. Just look everywhere." Callie looked by the swings and under the slide. Then she walked over to some bushes. She saw a little space on the ground under one bush.

"Jason, come here!" she called. "Look at this."

Jason got down on his hands and knees to look closely. "Hey! I think I see some fur!" he exclaimed.

Chapter Five

Callie was jumping up and down. "Miss Kitty, is that you? Be careful not to scare her, Jason."

Jason slowly reached his hand into the space and pulled it back out. He opened his hand and showed Callie a puff of black fur.

"Miss Kitty was here! That's her fur," Callie said.

"But where did she go from here?" Jason wondered.

"Maybe she went to the creek. Let's look there. Then we need to hang up the flyers."

⌘~⌘~⌘

Miss Kitty was not at the creek. So they headed back into town and stopped at a telephone pole. They worked their way up and down the street, stopping almost every block to hang up a flyer.

They had put up half the flyers when Callie had an idea. "We need to make a list of all the places we go so we don't just go around in circles," she suggested. "Do you have a pen or paper?"

"We've got all the paper we need." Jason held up the flyers. "But no pen. If we stop at the soda shop, they can give us one. We can have a drink, too," he said.

So they rode off in the direction of the soda shop. Callie was thankful Jason had suggested the soda shop. She really could use a drink and the rest. Maybe she wasn't feeling as well as she thought she was. And the peanut butter toast was wearing off.

Callie looked at every house and every porch on the way. She hoped to see some sign of her big black cat. But she found nothing.

"Maybe I should call Mom and let her know where we are," Callie said to Jason as they got on their bikes after hanging up another flyer.

"Sure, here. You take the walkie-talkie,"

Jason said, handing the radio to Callie.

"Mom? Mom, are you there?" Callie said into the small black box. "It's Callie. Can you hear me?"

"Sure can. Was Miss Kitty at the school playground?" Mom's voice came through.

"No," Callie answered. "But we found some of her fur."

"Where are y'all now?" Mom asked.

"Almost to the soda shop. We're going to stop for a drink and see if Mrs. Porter will let us have a pen to write down where we've been." Callie filled her mom in on their plan.

"That's a good idea," Mom said. "You and Jason get a snack, too. Remember, you have money on account there. All you do is sign the bill. OK?"

"OK, Mom," Callie answered.

"Make sure Jason gets something to eat. I know he must be hungry. It's almost one o'clock," Mom said.

"I will," Callie said. " 'Bye."

" 'Bye, sweetie. Good luck!" Mom called back. "I hope you find her real soon."

Callie and Jason rode their bikes up the long

hill to the soda shop. There weren't very many people in the shop. Mrs. Porter was behind the counter. Mr. Moore, whose daughter Jordan was in Callie's dance class, was at a table in the back.

Mr. Moore was the man who put up all the streetlights in town and did all the electric work for the school. Callie knew that he drove all over town in his big power truck. Maybe she could ask him to keep an eye out for Miss Kitty.

"Hi, you two! What brings you my way this afternoon?" Mrs. Porter asked Callie and Jason as they walked up to the counter.

"Good afternoon, Mrs. Porter. We're out looking for Callie's cat. You haven't seen her, have you?" Jason asked, sitting down at the counter.

"I'm sorry, Callie, but I haven't. But I will pass the word to everyone to be on the lookout for her," Mrs. Porter said, taking Callie's hand into hers.

"Thank you, Mrs. Porter," Callie said. "Could you hang up this flyer in the shop?"

"Why, I'd be happy to," Mrs. Porter said. "I'll put it right here on the counter where everyone will see it. Now, what can I get for you?"

"Mom said we could have something to eat, 'cause we've been looking all morning," Callie told the pretty lady. Mrs. Porter had long brown hair that she always wore in a braid. Callie wished her hair would do that. Then again, she wished her hair would do anything.

"Sure thing. What would you like?" Mrs. Porter asked.

"Can I have a ham and cheese sandwich and a Coke?" Jason asked.

"No problem. Miss Callie, what would you like?" Mrs. Porter turned to Callie.

"I think I'd like a grilled cheese sandwich and a Coke. Oh, and do you have a pen Jason and I could use?" Callie asked.

"Sure, honey," Mrs. Porter said, reaching under the counter. "Here you go. I'll have your sandwiches ready in a jiffy."

"Thank you," Callie called to her as she went into the kitchen.

Turning to face the window, Callie could see across the street to Dr. Gayle Aughtry's office. Dr. Gayle was the town's veterinarian. *After we eat,* Callie thought, *we need to go over there to see if anybody has brought Miss Kitty to her.*

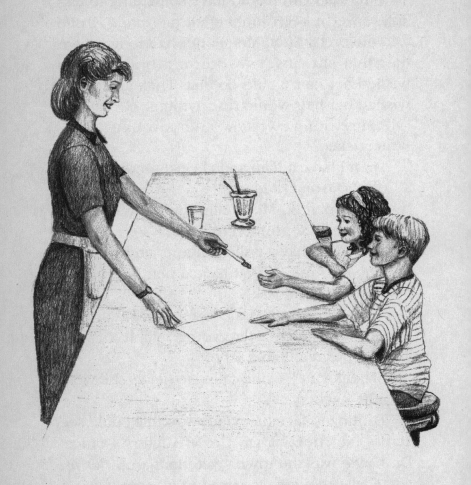

Turning back around, Callie saw Mr. Moore was still sitting at a table in the back.

"Jason, I'll be right back. I'm going to talk to Mr. Moore."

Chapter Six

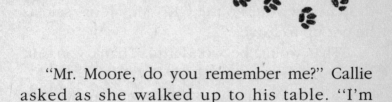

"Mr. Moore, do you remember me?" Callie asked as she walked up to his table. "I'm Reverend Davies' daughter, Callie."

"Sure, I do. What can I do for you?" Mr. Moore smiled and leaned forward.

"Well, you see, I know you drive all over town while you're working. I was wondering if you'd keep an eye out for my cat. She's missing," Callie said.

"I'd be happy to, Callie. What does she look like?" Mr. Moore asked.

"It would be hard to miss her. She has long black hair. And she weights about twenty-two pounds now," Callie said.

"Twenty-two pounds! My goodness! It would

be hard to miss her. What did you say her name was?" Mr. Moore asked.

"Her name's Miss Kitty. Here's a flyer about her. She'll come to you if you call her," Callie said. "She's a good cat. She doesn't bite or claw or anything."

"I'll keep an eye out for her. If I see her, I'll drop her by your house. OK?" Mr. Moore said as he got up to leave.

"That would be wonderful. Thank you, Mr. Moore. I hope you see her."

Callie joined Jason at the counter again. "Mr. Moore is going to look for Miss Kitty, too," she told him. "After we eat, I think we need to go over to Dr. Gayle's office to see if she's heard anything."

"Good idea. We could stop by and see if anybody at my aunt Gail's store has seen her," Jason added.

"I never noticed till now that your aunt and Dr. Aughtry have the same first name," Callie said.

"Yeah. But they have different spellings," Jason pointed out. "My aunt spells it G-a-i-l. Dr. Aughtry spells it G-a-y-l-e."

"Oh." Callie thought about it a minute. "I saw your aunt walking her dog the other day. What's his name?" Callie picked up the Coke Mrs. Porter brought out and took a big drink.

"Shyla is a girl. Aunt Gail just got her. Shyla thinks she can sit in your lap, but she's way too big for that," Jason said.

Jason went on about Shyla the dog. But all the while, Callie was thinking of all the places Miss Kitty could be. Callie and Jason always took her when they went on bike rides. So she had seen almost all of Cornelius. She could be anywhere.

Mrs. Porter brought out the sandwiches. Jason and Callie ate their lunches, then wrote down all the places they should go to look for the missing Miss Kitty.

"Thank you for the pen, Mrs. Porter. Lunch was real good," Callie said as they got up to leave.

"You are very welcome. I'll keep everyone posted on Miss Kitty. Let me know when you find her," Mrs. Porter called as Jason and Callie went out the door.

Callie and Jason were putting on their

helmets when Mr. Moore drove up in his truck. "Callie, someone just told me he was out by the creek this morning. He thought he saw a black cat when he was there. Maybe it was your Miss Kitty."

"OH, THANK YOU, MR. MOORE!" Callie had to shout, she was so excited. "Did you hear that, Jason? Let's go. Maybe she's still there. Hurry!" Callie jumped on her bike and pedaled off, hoping Jason would follow.

When they reached the creek, they left their bikes to look around for any clues. "Here, Miss Kitty! Where are you?" Callie called.

"Look over here, Callie," Jason said. He pointed in the dirt.

Callie leaned over to look closely at the ground.

Paw prints!

Chapter Seven

"What do you think?" Jason asked, peering closely at the tracks. "Are they Miss Kitty's?"

Callie was so excited she almost couldn't talk. "They could be. They're the right size. Are there more?"

Jason pushed away some weeds. "Nope. Just these few tracks right here."

"OH NO!" Callie cried. "She was here. I know it, Jason. Now we really have to find her."

"I still think we should check the bell tower at the church," Jason said.

"Jason, there's no way she could be there," Callie said, rolling her eyes. "Let's go see Dr. Gayle. We can leave a flyer there."

"Maybe somebody brought Miss Kitty to her," Jason suggested.

Callie tried not to cry the whole way back to town. They put their bikes in the rack next to the door that said *Dr. Gayle Aughtry, Veterinarian*, and entered the old two-story building.

"Hey, you two! What brings you my way?" Dr. Gayle got up from her desk to give Callie and Jason a hug.

"We were hoping you had seen my cat," Callie told the tall red-haired lady and handed her a flyer. Callie loved Dr. Gayle. She always made a fuss over Callie, and that made Callie feel really special. Dr. Gayle always told Callie, "We redheads have to stick together."

"Oh no, sweetie, I haven't. How long has she been gone?" Dr. Gayle asked, sitting down again in her big office chair.

"Well, I let her out yesterday morning really early. When Daddy went to get her, he couldn't find her. Do you think she's all right? I mean, without food or water for that long." Callie was almost crying again.

"Oh, darling, cats will find food and water. I'm sure she's all right," Dr. Gayle said. "She may just be out hunting. Cats will do that. I'll put a flyer on the phone up front. And I'll have Debbie ask everyone who comes in if they have seen her." She hugged Callie tight.

"Thank you, Dr. Gayle. I really miss her," Callie said.

"I know you do, honey. I'm sure you'll find her soon. Why don't you and Jason go by the police station and talk to Chief Aughtry? Maybe while he's making his rounds he can look, too." Police Chief Aughtry was Dr. Gayle's husband. "And be sure to leave one of your flyers with him."

"Good idea," Jason said. "Come on, Callie. Time's a-wasting."

"Thank you, Dr. Gayle. See you at Sunday school in the morning," Callie called back.

"See you then." Dr. Gayle waved as they went out the door.

"I guess we need to cross back over if we're going to the police station," Jason said as they got their bikes from the rack and put on their helmets.

"Yeah, I guess so," Callie said.

Walking the bikes back across the street,

Callie saw David and Jenni Wilson coming their way.

"Hey, you two! Where are you going?" David called.

"Hi, Jenni. Hi, David. We just came from Dr. Gayle's office. Now we're going to the police station to see Chief Aughtry. Dr. Gayle said he would look for Miss Kitty while he was making his rounds," Callie told her brother. "And we're going to put these flyers on the telephone poles as we go."

"Good idea, Callie. We've been by the school and down by the creek. Are there any other places you want us to look?" Jenni asked Callie.

"You could go back toward our house and go by the ball field," Callie said.

"We're on our way," David said. "We'll meet you two back home. And, Callie, check in with Mom every now and then. She's worried that you still don't feel too well."

"I will, David. Thank you for helping look for Miss Kitty, Jenni."

"Happy to do it, Callie. I know you'd help me if I needed it." Jenni gave Callie the thumbs-up and started back toward the ball field and

Callie's house with David.

Jason and Callie started up the street to see Chief Aughtry at his office in the police station.

"We could stop by my aunt Gail's shop now before we go the police station," Jason said. It was only a few doors down from the soda shop. Jason's aunt was a decorator. She had helped Callie's mom pick out the new drapes for the living room and the ones for Callie's room at their new house. Jason stuck his head in the door of the shop.

"Aunt Gail, you here?" Jason yelled at the top of his lungs.

"Why, yes, I am. Come on in. Hello, Callie, how are you?" the woman asked.

"Not real good, Miss Alexander. My cat, Miss Kitty, is missing. We've been out looking for her all day," Callie reported.

"Well, I sure am sorry, honey. I'll tell you what. I'm almost ready to go. I'll take the long way home and look as I go," Aunt Gail offered. "I'm sure Shyla will love the walk. Maybe I'll spot her for you. What does she look like?"

"Well, she's a big cat—twenty-two pounds with long black hair. Her name is Miss Kitty."

Callie handed her a flyer with Miss Kitty's picture on it.

"Aunt Gail," Jason said, "where is Shyla?"

"Oh, she was being a bad dog. She ate a set of new shades I just got in. So I put her in her pen for a while." Aunt Gail gave Jason a hug. "Tell your dad and mom I said hello. I'll see them tomorrow at church."

"I will. 'Bye, Aunt Gail," Jason said.

"We'd better hurry, Jason. It's almost three-thirty. Mom won't let me stay out much longer," Callie said.

Callie and Jason headed for the police station. Callie was getting tired, but she was not going to give up. Miss Kitty was out there somewhere, and Callie was going to find her—even if it took all night!

"I wonder if the chief is even here today," Callie said as they walked in the front door of the police station.

"Sure, he's here. I saw his truck outside," Jason said, pulling Callie down the long hall to the office of Police Chief Aughtry.

"Hello, you two. Dr. Gayle called and said you'd be stopping by. Callie, can you tell me what your cat looks like? I'll have the other officers look for her as they make their rounds." Chief Aughtry had come out of his office and was walking down the hall to meet them.

"Well, she's big—about twenty-two pounds—and she has long black hair. And she has a red collar with a bell on it so she can't get to the birds," Callie said. "Here's a flyer with her picture on it. It might help."

"At twenty-two pounds, we can't miss her, that's for sure. Will she come if you call her name?" Chief Aughtry asked.

"Oh yes, sir. And she won't bite or claw or anything. She's a real good cat. Just big, that's all. Please ask your officers to look out for her. Jake won't be with you while you're looking, will he?" Callie asked in an uncertain voice. Jake was the Aughtrys' dog, and Callie knew he liked to chase cats.

"Oh no, Jake is over with Dr. Gayle today. He's baby-sitting a new puppy," Chief Aughtry assured them. "Jake likes to take care of any lost pups."

Suddenly, Callie heard her name come over the walkie-talkie in Jason's hand.

"Callie, are you there?" Mom's voice said.

Jason handed Callie the walkie-talkie.

"Yes, Mom, I'm here. We're at the police station talking to Chief Aughtry. He's going to help look for Miss Kitty," Callie said into the radio.

"That's wonderful. You two need to start home now. It's getting late and I don't want you out. Supper will be in an hour or so," Callie's mom commanded.

"But, Mom," Callie started, "I need—"

"No buts, Callie Ann," Mom cut in. "You two start home. You can look as you come this way. David has some of his friends out looking now."

"If David can stay out, why can't I?" Callie asked in her best whiny voice.

"Callie, do I need to come pick you up?" Mom asked in a stern voice.

"No, ma'am. We're on our way. See you in a little while," Callie said.

"Let's go, Jason. I really don't want Mom and Daddy mad at me now," Callie told Jason. "Thank you, Chief Aughtry, for all your help."

"No problem. I'll call if we find her. Don't worry, Callie. I'm sure somebody will find her."

Chief Aughtry walked Callie and Jason to the front door.

Callie and Jason didn't talk all the way home. It was all Callie could do to ride her bike. Turning onto their street, they saw Jason's mom and dad outside.

"I wonder what they're doing?" Jason said.

"I don't know. Looks like they're looking for something," Callie said.

Jason and Callie pulled their bikes into Jason's driveway and found Callie's mom and daddy there, too.

"What are y'all doing?" Jason asked, taking off his bike helmet.

Mrs. Alexander put an arm around each of them. "Jason, Callie, now Jack is missing, too."

Oh no! Callie thought. *First Miss Kitty. And now Jack!*

Chapter Eight

Mrs. Alexander explained what happened. "I let him go on the back porch, and the next thing I knew he was gone. Your dad and I have been looking for him. So have Reverend and Mrs. Davies."

"Holy smoke! He's looking for Miss Kitty, too." Jason sat down on the ground and put his hands on his head.

"Oh, Jason, I'm so sorry. I didn't mean for Jack to come up missing, too." Callie began to cry again.

"Oh, Callie, don't cry," Jason said, getting up to put his arm around Callie. "I'm sure Jack will find her and bring her home. Jack has been out

before. He'll come back and bring Miss Kitty with him."

"Do you really think so, Jason? Do you think Jack can find her?" Callie asked.

"Yep! I'm sure of it. Jack is smart, just like me!" Jason smiled. "You have the other walkie-talkie at your house. I'll let you know as soon as Jack comes back in, OK?" Jason offered.

"OK, Jason. I'll talk to you later," Callie said.

Callie and her parents said good-bye to the Alexanders and went across the yard to their house. Callie was really worried now. First, Miss Kitty was gone. And now Jack. What if somebody had taken them? But why would somebody want Miss Kitty and Jack?

Mom had fixed one of Callie's favorites—hot dogs with chili and onions—for supper. But Callie just couldn't eat. She was too upset to do anything.

"Mom, I think I'll go take a shower and go to bed. I don't feel too good," Callie said, getting up from the table.

"OK, honey, I'll be up after you take your shower," Mom said. "Are you sure you don't want anything else to eat?"

"I don't think so, Mom," Callie said, giving her a weak smile.

Callie went up to her room. Looking around, all she could see were things that reminded her of Miss Kitty. Her bed. The cat brush. The window seat. Callie sat down on the bed.

"Dear God," she prayed. "It's me, Callie. We looked all day, and I still can't find Miss Kitty. Can you please help? I just want her to come back home. And now Jack's missing, too. Look after them, wherever they are. Bless everyone I know and even those I don't. Amen."

❧❧❧

Callie had taken her shower and was sitting at the window seat when the walkie-talkie came on.

"Callie, are you there?" came Jason's voice.

Callie picked up the radio. "Yeah, I'm here, Jason. I'm so sorry Jack is missing, too. I wonder if he and Miss Kitty are together," she said.

"Well, I don't know. But I do know that Jack likes Miss Kitty. He might have been worried about her, too," Jason answered.

"You know what?" Callie asked.

"What?"

"You are OK for a boy." Callie laughed for the first time in days. She was still worried about Miss Kitty. But she was glad to know that she had a good friend in Jason Alexander.

"Jason, do you think we looked everywhere today? I mean, can you think of anyplace we didn't go?" Callie asked.

"I can't think of anyplace. OH, WAIT!" Jason said in a loud voice. "Did we go by Masons' store?"

"No, we didn't. Should I call over there to ask if they've seen her?" Callie asked.

"It couldn't hurt. Ask for Bobby. He works at the store on Saturdays. Maybe he was out back and saw her," Jason said. "Will you call me back, or do you want me to stay on the walkie-talkie?"

"Just stay on. I'll be right back!" Callie jumped up from the window seat. She went into the hall where the phone was and dialed the Masons' number.

"Hello, is Bobby home? This is Callie

Davies," Callie said when Bobby's dad answered the phone.

"Hello," Bobby said in a deep voice.

"Bobby, hi, it's Callie. Were you at the store today with your mom and dad?" Callie asked.

"No, I went to Charlotte with my aunt Mary. Why?" Bobby asked.

"Well, Miss Kitty's missing, and so is Jason's cat, Jack. I thought if you had been at the store you might have seen them," Callie explained.

"Sorry, Callie. But I'll help you look after church if you still haven't found her," Bobby offered.

"Thank you, Bobby. I hope we find her before that. See you in the morning." Callie hung up the phone and went back into her bedroom.

"Jason, you there?" Callie asked into the small black box.

"I'm here. Any luck?" Jason asked.

"No, Bobby was in Charlotte all day. Can you think of anybody else?" Callie asked.

"No, I can't. Maybe we can think better in the morning," Jason said. "I need to get to bed now, Callie. I'll see you in the morning. Good night."

"Good night, Jason. Thank you." Callie set the radio down and climbed into bed.

Chapter Nine

Callie couldn't sleep. She was awake for what seemed to be forever. So she got up and sat on the window seat for a while. Jason was sitting in his window, too.

"Hey," the black box beside Callie said.

"Hey," Callie said back. "You can't sleep, either?"

"Nope. I wonder if Jack and Miss Kitty are safe," Jason said.

"Well, I asked God to keep them safe. I know we looked everywhere, but I can't help thinking that we missed somewhere," Callie said.

"I know, me too. I wish we could go out and find them now," Jason said.

"Jason, it's eleven-thirty. I don't think your

mom or mine will let us out the door." Callie sighed. "And besides that, we really need to go to sleep. So I'm getting off and going to sleep. You do the same!"

"Boy, you're bossy. Night, Cal."

"Night, Jason." Callie waved from the window.

Callie finally fell asleep. But she had a very restless night. Miss Kitty was in her dreams. Where could she be? Callie and Jason had looked everywhere. They had even gone by the creek twice.

❧❧❧

When Callie woke up, she thought that maybe it had all been a bad dream. Maybe Miss Kitty was really still in the house. But Callie got out of bed and could see that it had not been a dream. Miss Kitty was still missing.

"Mom," Callie called down the stairs. "What time is it? My clock stopped at one o'clock last night."

"It's eight-twenty-five, Callie," Mom called back up the steps. "Time to get ready for church.

Would you like blueberry pancakes for breakfast?"

"Sure, that sounds real good," Callie said as she came into the kitchen.

"How are you feeling this morning, Callie?" Daddy asked as Callie plopped down in a chair at the table.

"Sad, unhappy, mad, upset. You name it, I feel it," Callie answered.

"Oh my, all that?" Daddy said, hugging Callie.

"Yes, sir. I'm mad at me for letting her go out without me. And I'm upset with me for not finding her yesterday."

"Honey, you can't be mad at yourself for that," Daddy said. "We all looked for her and didn't find her. And she had to go out. You couldn't have stopped that."

But Callie was still mad at herself. And now Jack was gone, too. What if he got lost trying to find Miss Kitty?

"Morning, Callie," David said, coming into the kitchen to eat breakfast. "Jenni and I are going to ask the Sunday school class to help us look after church today. I'm sure we'll find her.

I can just feel it. Miss Kitty will be back." David picked up Callie from her chair and swung her around the kitchen.

"Thank you, David. But now we have another missing cat. Jack's gone, too," Callie said when David put her down.

"We'll find him, too. He's just out looking for his buddy, that's all. When we find her, we'll find him. I just know it." David sat down to eat his pancakes.

Callie ate her pancakes without saying much. All she could think of was the missing cats and what David had said. Maybe today would be the day. Maybe Miss Kitty would be on the back porch when they came home from church, and Jack would be right there with her.

"Callie, you need to stop daydreaming and eat so you can get dressed," Mom said.

When Callie finished eating, she went back to her room to get dressed for church.

"You need to hurry, Callie," Daddy said as Callie was trying to pull her hair back. "We're going to be late."

"I'm almost ready, Daddy. I'm already dressed. And I'm pulling my hair back now."

Mom came into Callie's room. "Here, let me help you. We are really running late today. We should have been at the church twenty minutes ago."

Five minutes later, they were on the way to church. All the way there, Callie looked out the car window for Miss Kitty.

When they arrived, Callie found Jason by the door to the church.

"Hi, Jason. Did Jack come home yet?" Callie asked.

"No, he's not back yet. I asked around, but nobody has seen our cats," Jason said. "But they'll be home soon. I just have a feeling."

"David said the same thing this morning. I hope y'all are right. I really miss them both," Callie said as they walked into church.

Sunday school was all about how you should never give up hope. Callie thought about that. She had almost given up.

But David and Jason had hope. They said they still believed that both cats would come home.

Leaving the Sunday school class for the morning service, Callie really began to have hope again. Miss Kitty would come home. And it would be today.

Callie's mom was sitting about halfway up to the front. Callie went to join her. Jason sat with his parents behind Callie and her mom.

Callie's daddy stood before the congregation with his Bible open. First, he told everyone that Miss Kitty and Jack were missing. He asked everyone to pray that the cats be found. Then he started his sermon.

But he stopped after just a few sentences. He was looking at something at the back of the church.

All of a sudden something jumped on the pew beside Callie.

Miss Kitty!

Chapter Ten

"OH, MISS KITTY! WHERE HAVE YOU BEEN?" Callie yelled right in the middle of church. She noticed something in Miss Kitty's mouth. "What do you have?"

Miss Kitty dropped a small bundle of black fur in Callie's lap.

A kitten!

Then Miss Kitty jumped down and started back up the aisle. But she stopped and meowed at Jason really loud.

"Wait, Miss Kitty, where are you going?" Callie said, getting up to follow. She handed the kitten to her mom. "Oh, Daddy. I'm sorry. I have to go after her. Come on, Jason."

"Go ahead, Callie. I'd like to know where

she's going myself." Daddy stepped down from the pulpit and started up the aisle.

"Wait, Miss Kitty," Callie called after the big black cat.

Miss Kitty went up the steps to the bell tower. She went through a small hole at one side of the door.

By then, Jason had caught up with them. "Where did she go, Callie?" he asked.

"The bell tower," Callie said, pushing the door open. "She went in through the hole at the side of the door."

And there in the bell tower were Miss Kitty, Jack, and three more kittens. Two were white—just like Jack. And the other kitten was black—just like the one Miss Kitty had brought to Callie downstairs.

"Mom!" Callie yelled downstairs. "Come look. Miss Kitty's had kittens. Four of them. In the bell tower, just like where she was born in Greenville. Oh, Mom, they are so cute."

Callie's mom and daddy came up the stairs and joined them.

"Well, just look, Miss Kitty and Jack have a family," Daddy said. "Well, now that we know

she's all right, I think we'll have our church service. And before you even ask, Callie, yes, you may stay with her until after church. Then we'll find a box and take the new family home."

After asking permission, Jason stayed with Callie and the cats, too. He got a small bowl from the church kitchen and brought some water up for Miss Kitty and Jack.

"I wonder if they're hungry," Jason said.

"Look, Jason. This one looks just like Jack. He's all white with a little dot of black on his tail!" Callie exclaimed. "I think they can wait to eat until we get them home. It won't be long now. And, Jason, I'm sorry."

"For what?" Jason looked confused.

"You said yesterday we should look in the bell tower. And I told you there was no way she could be up here."

Callie put the little white kitten back beside Miss Kitty. "If we had, they would have been home instead of spending the night here in the bell tower."

"Oh, well, Callie. Don't worry about it. We found them, and they're all right now," Jason assured her. "Hey, now we're related! You're a grandma, and I'm a grandpa." He laughed.

"Just wait until Meg hears about this," Callie said. "She'll love it. Maybe I can give my grand-mama and grandpapa a kitten. Is that all right with you?"

"Fine with me. I'd like to keep one if my mom and dad will let me," Jason said, rubbing Jack. "You're a good boy, Jack. You stayed with Miss Kitty just to make sure she was all right."

"Yeah, and just like you said, something good happened today. God answered my prayer and gave us four new cats as a bonus." Callie laughed and held up one of the kittens into the warm sunlight.

Oh boy, four new cats, Callie thought. *What a weekend this has been.*

Series for Young Readers*
From Bethany House Publishers

★ ★ ★

THE ADVENTURES OF CALLIE ANN
by Shannon Mason Leppard

Readers will giggle their way through the true-to-life escapades of Callie Ann Davies and her many North Carolina friends.

★ ★ ★

BACKPACK MYSTERIES
by Mary Carpenter Reid

This excitement-filled mystery series follows the mishaps and adventures of Steff and Paulie Larson as they strive to help often-eccentric relatives crack their toughest cases.

★ ★ ★

THE CUL-DE-SAC KIDS
by Beverly Lewis

Each story in this lighthearted series features the hilarious antics and predicaments of nine endearing boys and girls who live on Blossom Hill Lane.

★ ★ ★

RUBY SLIPPERS SCHOOL
by Stacy Towle Morgan

Join the fun as home-schoolers Hope and Annie Brown visit fascinating countries and meet inspiring Christians from around the world!

★ ★ ★

THREE COUSINS DETECTIVE CLUB®
by Elspeth Campbell Murphy

Famous detective cousins Timothy, Titus, and Sarah-Jane learn compelling Scripture-based truths while finding—and solving—intriguing mysteries.

* (ages 7–10)